This book belongs to:

_____

Digital art by Callaway Animation Studios under the direction of David Kirk in collaboration
with Nelvana Limited.

This book is based on the TV episode "Eight Legs Up," written by Alice Prodanou, from the animated TV series
Miss Spider's Sunny Patch Friends on Nick Jr., a Nelvana Limited/Absolute Pictures Limited
co-production in association with Callaway Arts & Entertainment,
based on the Miss Spider books by David Kirk.

Nicholas Callaway, President and Publisher
Cathy Ferrara, Managing Editor and Production Director
Toshiya Masuda, Art Director • Nelson Gomez, Director of Digital Services
Joya Rajadhyaksha, Associate Editor • Amy Cloud, Associate Editor
Raphael Shea, Senior Designer • Krupa Jhaveri, Designer
Bill Burg, Digital Artist • Christina Pagano, Digital Artist • Keith McMenamy, Digital Artist

Special thanks to the Nelvana staff, including Doug Murphy, Scott Dyer, Tracy Ewing, Pam Lehn,
Tonya Lindo, Mark Picard, Jane Sobol, Luis Lopez, Eric Pentz, and Georgina Robinson.

Library of Congress Cataloging-in-Publication Data available upon request.

Distributed in the United States by Viking Children's Books.

Callaway Arts & Entertainment, its Callaway logotype,
and Callaway & Kirk Company LLC are trademarks.

ISBN 0-448-44517-4

Visit Callaway Arts & Entertainment at www.callaway.com

10 9 8 7 6 5 4 3 2 1 06 07 08 09 10

Printed in China

Miss Spider's
SUNNY PATCH FRIENDS

Eight Legs Up

David Kirk

CALLAWAY

NEW YORK

2006

The Sunny Patch Pinecone Derby was in a few days. Bounce and Snowdrop were trying out for the running team.

"On your mark, get set . . . GO!" Mr. Mantis yelled.

Snowdrop huffed and puffed, but she couldn't run very fast. She turned a corner and all of a sudden . . .

She crashed into a little green beetle!

"I'm so sorry!" Snowdrop cried.

"Wow, you have eight legs!" exclaimed the dizzy beetle. "That's a lot!"

"I-I guess I do have a lot of legs," Snowdrop stammered.

Back home, Snowdrop sadly told Miss Spider what happened. "I can't be in the Derby because I have too many legs! That's why I'm so clumsy."

"But Snowdrop," Miss Spider soothed, "spiders are *supposed* to have eight legs."

The rest of the bugs zipped into the Cozy Hole, buzzing about the Pinecone Derby. Dragon had made the flying team. Squirt and Pansy were going to surf their webs.

"And I'm the fastest runner on two legs!" Bounce laughed.

Maybe two legs are better than eight! Snowdrop thought.

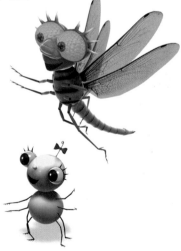

The next day, Snowdrop tied six of her legs behind her back and wobbled into the meadow.

"Snowdrop, what happened to your legs?" Squirt asked.

"Eight legs were just too many," Snowdrop replied. "Now I have two legs, just like Bounce!"

"But spiders are supposed to have eight legs," said Bounce.

"I walk better with only two," Snowdrop replied. As she wobbled away, she tripped over an acorn.

"Oomph! Then again, maybe six legs would be better."

Snowdrop tied two sets of legs together.

"Six legs are faster than eight!" she declared, shakily crawling along. "Right, Dragon?"

"Dragonflies have six legs," said Dragon, "but we're only fast when we fly."

That's it! I need some wings, thought Snowdrop as she fell to the ground.

19

Next, Snowdrop tied big leaves to two of her legs just as Shimmer flew overhead.

"Now I have six legs and two wings—like you, Shimmer!" she said.

"But I'm a beetle," said Shimmer. "Spiders don't fly."

"Just watch me!" bragged Snowdrop.

Snowdrop leapt off a tree stump into the air. Flapping her wings, she struggled to stay aloft, but soon crashed to the ground.

"Snowdrop, are you all right?" Shimmer cried.

"I think I sprained a couple of ankles," moaned Snowdrop miserably.

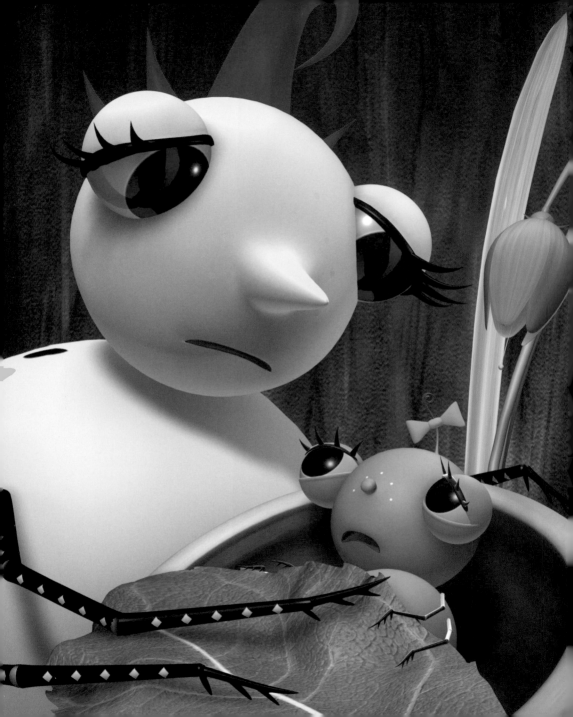

B ack at the Cozy Hole, Miss Spider bandaged Snowdrop's ankles and put her into bed.

"I'm clumsy no matter how many legs I have," Snowdrop sniffled.

"I think I know how to show Snowdrop how graceful she is," said Holley after they left the room.

Miss Spider and Holley returned to the kids' bedroom.

"Snowdrop, look at this picture of Pansy at her dance recital last year," Holley said.

Snowdrop stared at the photo wistfully. "We may be twins, but Pansy isn't clumsy at all."

"Look closer," Holley told her.

"Hey! That's my green bow!" Snowdrop exclaimed. "It's not Pansy—it's me!"

"Everybuggy thought you danced so beautifully that night," Miss Spider told her. "They said you were very talented."

"I guess eight legs isn't too many," Snowdrop said.

"Not for a spider," Holley said.

"Some bugs have six legs, and others have two," Miss Spider explained. "We're all special in a different way!"

The next day, Snowdrop and her parents cheered for the other bugs at the Derby. Afterward, Mr. Mantis gave each bug a special medal.

"I don't have enough hands!" he exclaimed.

"I'll help," said Snowdrop. "I have eight!"

Everybuggy laughed.